P9-BIZ-308

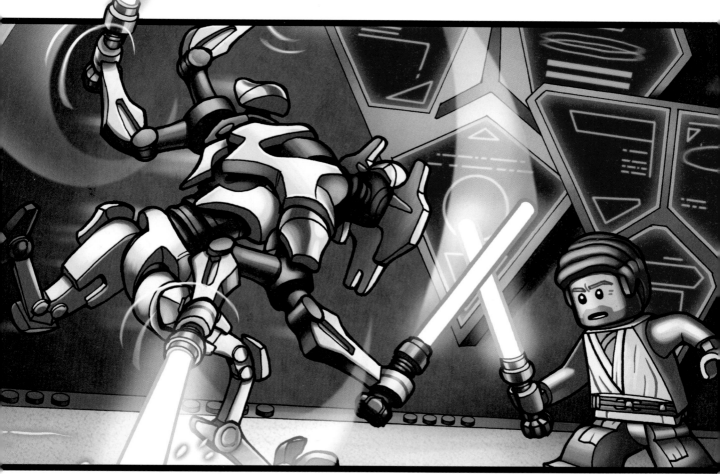

LA VENGANZA DE LOS SITH

ACE LANDERS   ILUSTRADO POR DAVID WHITE

SCHOLASTIC INC.

Originally published in English as Lego Star Wars: Revenge of the Sith

LEGO, the LEGO logo, the Brick and Knob configurations and the Minifigure are trademarks of the LEGO Group. © 2016 The LEGO Group. Produced by Scholastic Inc. under license from the LEGO Group.

Published by Scholastic Inc. Publishers since 1920. scholastic, scholastic en español, and associated logos are trademarks and/or registered trademarks of Scholastic Inc.

ISBN 978-0-545-90355-4

10 9 8 7 6 5 4   16 17 18 19 20

Printed in the U.S.A.   40
First Scholastic Spanish printing, January 2016

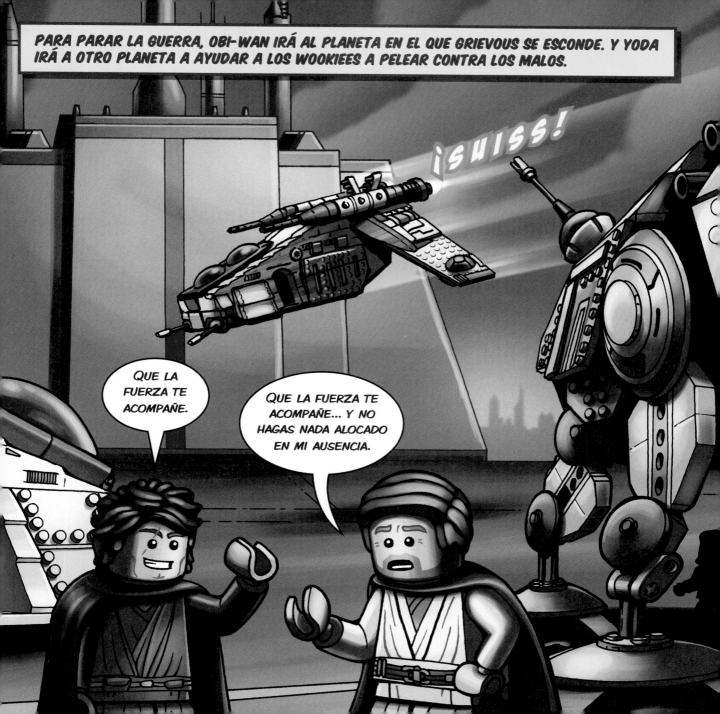